I0571012

The Blue Wind Whispers to Me in the Moment of Fear: Collection of
Short and Micro Stories from When I Didn't
Know Any Better

By Ari Meier

Viori Publishing
P.O. Box 5283
Atlanta, GA 31107
http://vioripublishing.com

You may contact Ari Meier at Viori Publishing at
ari@vioripublishing.com

Published by Viori Publishing

ISBN 978-0-9913432-0-1

PRINTED IN THE UNITED STATES OF AMERICA

Special thanks

To the love of my life Violette, thank you for your great ideas, patience, and support.

To my late mom, Margaret Rose, thank you for your guidance, love and nurturing and for creating an environment that allowed me to write freely and often.

Preface

Many of these stories were written between the ages 14-25. They've only been edited for grammar and not content and ideas. Please enjoy.

Contents

Terror, 17 Floors up

The day started off as nice, hot and humid; by 7:30 the sky began to get cloudy. I called my friend Willie at 8:30 to see if he wanted to hang downtown. He came over to my house at 8:47 and we left immediately. We walked around, going into several stores.

The clouds got thicker and the time is 9:06. It began to rain. We were in the 700 block of the widest street in Augusta, GA or for that matter, in the world, excluding Canal Street in New Orleans. We stood under the "front porch" of the stately Southern Financial Empire Building, Augusta's tallest building.

Rain was coming down harder by now with the wind blowing stronger. I saw sheet lightning and heard thunder in the distance. I said, "Willie, let's go into the Southern Financial Empire Building until the rain and lightning cool down." He said, "You're crazy, we should run home."

I went inside anyway and Willie followed me in. The time is 9:16. The inside of the building is contrastingly modern compared to the outside. While we were inside, I started walking up the stairs. Willie asked, "Why don't we go home?" I told him, "I'm not getting wet and taking a chance with the lightning; but you can."

As Willie followed me up the stairs to the fourth floor, I could hear thunder through the walls of the eerily quiet building. We climbed up more flights of stairs until we reached the 16th and formerly the old building's top floor. We walked out into the dark hallway; as I scrambled to find a light switch, I heard a faint scream. I asked Willie if he heard the scream; he replied that he hadn't.

The time is 9:23. I wondered aloud how we could get up to the penthouse. Willie then asked about the penthouse and why it was built. I told him about a former state senator having a dream about Jesus erecting a huge cross on the top of this building. This happened about ten years earlier, but instead, the senator erected the current penthouse and later added a huge lighted cross to the top of the penthouse. This penthouse served as the senator's residential and business base.

There was also a less publicized story about the senator's wife killing herself because of the senator's later fraud indictment case in which he was sentenced to prison. Many people spoke about the wife killing herself in the penthouse by hanging.

The time is 9:26 and the weather is getting worse, especially with the stronger winds which has a slight high pitched whistle.

I found a light switch at the other end of the dark hall and turned the lights on. The light revealed a much unattended hallway with paint peeling and stained carpet. There is a mildewy smell in the air and I hear the scream again! I whispered, "I definitely heard that Willie. It sounded like it came from the penthouse above." Willie jokingly said, "It might be the ghost of that lady who killed herself." I also had the same feeling, but not in a joking way. I kept quiet about it.

The thunder is rumbling louder. I see sharp lightning through the far office window. My eerie feelings about the suicide in the penthouse and screams were soon replaced with feelings of curiosity about the way the penthouse looked on the inside. As long as I could remember, I'd been fascinated with the design of the penthouse. I felt that the very modern, almost futuristic design contrasted with the neo gothic high rise building, but in a good way.

We walked around a corner and found some spiral stairs going up into a dark hole. I said, "Maybe that's the way to get inside the penthouse." As Willie started climbing the stairs, he almost slipped and a sudden chill ran through me.

The time is 9:41. We walked around the penthouse for a couple of minutes commenting on how well it was designed. Eerie feelings bubbled up about the penthouse being the location where the senator's wife hung herself and possibly being the source of the strange screams.

Although the dark penthouse is periodically lit up by lightning flashes, I couldn't help but to allow my imagination form images in the corners of the rooms and mirrors.

Before that loud thunder clap and close lightning strike, I knew that I saw something. A woman's body outline maybe? Or maybe a swinging rope over by the kitchen area. I forced my rational mind to conclude that I was just imagining all of this and that I heard or saw nothing!

I hear the scream again and know that Willie should have heard it. He did hear it.

We ran to the back of the penthouse, but Willie ran into something in the middle of the floor and fell. I ran back to see about him. He ran in to what looks like some sort of brick wall that's surrounding a small pool or water fountain.

He said that he couldn't move his right leg. He broke his leg! How would I be able to help him down 16 flights of stairs? He had to weigh at least 160 or 180 pounds. The idea of having to go very slow down 16 flights in a dark building with a possible ghost didn't feel good; it felt outright terrifying.

My increasingly scared mind started to look around for something to wrap Willie's leg with. I stumbled into a small door which I opened. There was something hanging in the dark room. It seemed to be a huge mobile sculpture.

With the next lightning flash, I saw something, but it wasn't a sculpture or any art. It was the body of a woman, partially decomposed and hanging from what looked like several nylon stockings tied around a ceiling beam. I felt something brush across my back. I turned around to see more dark. I turned to face the grotesque hanging lady. She was gone!

I felt a definite finger tip on my back and then what felt like hands around my neck. I ran. The creature held onto my neck, then letting go as I zigzagged through the dark penthouse. She let out an eerie scream. Willie tried getting up as I got to him, helping him limp run with me to the spiral staircase.

The thunder and lightning frequency is almost exaggerative. It comes with a frequency that seemed to be better fit for a bad horror film. I gripped the iron railing of the spiral staircase; it felt wet and almost syrupy like.

I smelled the mystery liquid; it smelled like iron, but not the iron railing kind of iron. It smelled like blood. With the next lightning strike, this liquid was confirmed to be blood.

The ghost woman's screams were almost rhythmic now.

The woman came towards us in a slow, but steady pace. It was hard and slow going down the spiral stairs with Willie's broken leg; but we reached the bottom and ran towards the main staircase. We froze in our tracks.

Our path was blocked by some shadowy figure. It was the ghost lady! How did she get down here so fast? We ran to the back of the building where the rooftop patio was and ran out onto the patio. We tried to go back into the building, but found her blocking the door. With the next lightning strike, I could see blood running down from her neck.

She came toward us chanting "all must die on the 4th of July". My mind raced for the logic or clue of what her words meant. I suddenly remembered that she killed herself on the 4th of July a couple of years back! Another thought hit me like a speeding car. Today is the 4th of July!

The time is 10:07. I thought about how we could get back into the building. I then ran around in a circle trying to confuse the ghost woman as Willie got on his one good foot. I helped him to limp and run through the door and back into the dark and dry building. I immediately locked the outside door.

As we ran and limped through the dark hallway, I looked ahead, at the moment when the next lightning strike lit up the dark corridor and saw the lady! This time she was soaked in blood. I turned around, the lightning lit up a wall. I saw a terrifying image of me and Willie dangling from the edge of the building. On the right side of the image were the words, "all must die on the 4th of July," written in blood.

The time is 10:18. It seems that the building is a huge puzzle-with the ghost lady at each corner. The screaming grew louder along with the thunder and wind. I felt something warm dripping on me. Blood! I looked up at the ceiling and in the dim light, saw what looked like an outline of Willie hanging from the ceiling. I looked around; calling for Willie, there was no sound of him! I ran towards the stairs, but they were not there. I ran to the elevator and got inside, hoping that it would work.

The elevator moved up, up and up. A button marked 20th stayed lit. Fear grew within like an explosion. There was no 20th floor in this building. Where was this elevator taking me? Where's Willie? The elevator stopped at the 20th floor, then down to the 15th floor, then almost to the 14th floor, and then stopped.

The elevator lights started dimming and then going completely out, then flickering almost like a disco light. I looked in the mirrored wall during the flickering and saw the ghost lady behind me. How did she get in the elevator?

She chanted, "All must die on the 4th of July." I moved away from her and pressed the 1st floor button repeatedly as she moved closer to me with outstretched arms. The elevator moved a little down to the 14th floor. The doors opened and I leaped out. I see Willie and he is walking normally!

I asked him where he disappeared to. He said, "I felt blood dripping on me and looked up to find you hanging from the ceiling. I thought you said this building only had 16 floors? I got on an elevator that took me up to the 20th floor! Man, this floor was the weirdest thing I've ever seen.

Where I thought the windows should be, there were sidewalks. I seriously thought I was on the ground and started on the sidewalks towards the window's edge, only to find as I got closer, there was a randomly flickering human like form near the window's edge with sock like things where its hands should be. This creature almost convinced me to keep walking on the sidewalk when I was pulled by this strong suction like wind onto the floor. I felt something touch my right leg and afterwards, my leg had an intense burning followed by itching. After all this, I felt that my leg was okay and walked on it."

The thunder is relentless. We run down the hallway and hear what sounds like voices that are mixed with a high pitched bird chirping sound. Again, I couldn't find the stairs! Had they disappeared?

How would we get out of this vertical puzzle? We rounded a corner. There's a whirring mechanical sound. The sound seems to be coming from the window on the right side. At the moment of the next lightning strike, I looked at the window and see an escalator going through it, but going outside to nothing!

We run down another hall and start to hear creaking sounds coming from the ceiling and walls. The building sounds as if it's in pain. Voices; I hear the voices again, but this time they're much closer. We run down another hallway and this hallway is crooked. It tilted throughout the entire length at differing angles. I felt dizzy going through this hallway. Where are the stairs?

There were no stairs! We went down another hallway. This hallway seems to be a mile long. As we neared the end, we see stairs! I felt something near my back as we ran. I turned around, but didn't see anything. I feel something, almost like a super cold knife at my shoulders.

The voices were louder and the cold knife feeling stayed with me. There is a mirrored section of the hallway by the stairs that revealed that the ghost woman was so close to me that she looked as if she was attached to me.

I couldn't get down the stairs fast enough. The staircase is dark. The ghost woman is on our backs and we have a ways to go to get down to the bottom. Willie leads the way down the stairs. My heart is pounding from the running and the fear that this woman creature is on me. With each turn on the staircase, I feel this cold envelope my back, my shoes and hair. The thought of this ghost this close to me and in the dark of the staircase unnerved me to no end.

We finally reached the first floor. The whole floor is a river of blood that came up to our knees. This is so crazy. Blood is running off the ceiling and dripping down the walls. The extreme cold left me half way down the blood hallway.

We reached the doors, but they wouldn't open. I thought that there must be some lock that we can turn to get out. There is none. The ghost woman was near the middle of the hallway, heading towards us. We tried to open the door again. It wouldn't budge!

The ghost woman's eyeballs fell out and out spilled a luminous yellow substance which fell into the blood. It transformed into a stringy vine-like globulous substance that came towards us in the blood river. I feel that this substance would do us great harm if it touched us because as it flowed through the blood river, the blood behind it evaporated. It started to get very hot and there is a strange sickening smell. We banged on the door, still attempting to get out.

We thought a couple of people outside of the building could hear us as they walked past the door. But they didn't seem to notice us. They seemed to change as they walked farther away. They were no longer three dimensional! They changed to a flat form as they walked farther from the building.

We banged and kicked the door. I kicked harder and harder. The door wouldn't budge. The yellow substance got closer and the putrid smell got stronger. The ghost woman is nowhere to be found. Willie said, "The blood is pulling up to the ceiling." I looked up and see the woman upside down on the ceiling. We suddenly found ourselves "falling" up to the ceiling. We landed on our feet, but it was not the ceiling. It was the floor! But how?

We somehow were upside down and landed right side up. We got our bearings and both kicked at the door. We kick harder and finally break through! We run through the broken glass, bleeding from our wounds, but these were our freedom wounds. I could care less about having to possibly need stitches.

We are free from that horrible building, with the creepy ghost woman, the piercing screams, the dark penthouse, and the otherworldly realms that defied gravity, time, space and logic. The time is 10:51.

The next morning, I awake to a beautiful day. I go downtown to see the building, my captor the previous night, and felt great fear wash through me and it was magnified when I looked up at the penthouse, which looked very serene, but frightening, all at the same time. I later read the newspaper and there was an article about the building. Seems that a New York based company just bought the building and they're going to add four more floors to the building; then it will have 20 floors!

Soul Bird

Oh God! How warm is the water? Laura began to flick water in my eyes as we took our weekly bath together. I plant a kiss on her right nipple as she caresses my thigh. Mmmm. Splashing water sounds mixed with blasts of New Age jazz is our, well, my idea of a serene Sunday night in the bath. While looking at my sweetheart, I think of all the special events preceding the bath. The tender and intense orgasmic moments. Yes. Mmmm. I feel drowsy as I pat-dry myself. Ready for bed. Laura is complaining about having to go home as usual.

After she leaves, I lie in my bed looking at the strange abstract patterns created by my window blinds. Sometimes I imagine drawing the pattern outlines on my ceiling. My eyes race around the dark apartment as my vivid imagination starts its fueling process. A process that starts with a simple hanging plant. A wall picture. Eyes are closing, drifting into the subconscious world.

I feel so heavy, as if gravity has increased tenfold. Walking along the side of interstate 85 while carrying my lunch and workout clothes. But I don't go to the spa on Wednesdays and don't need to go to Jupiter this year. Many birds are flying over me in my dark office at the IRS Building. I sit patiently waiting in my office because I'm looking for a certain bird.

This bird lands on my desk. It's a certain bird, not just any bird, it's a certain bird. I can't even tell you what it is about this bird that makes it go into the realm of 'certain bird'. I just know that this is the bird, I was looking for. This bird is not afraid of me or for that matter-anything. It stares at me. It moves its head in the curious head tilt way a perplexed dog's head would move.

I feel too light to stay in my seat. The bird is still looking at me as if it's scoring my every move. I float above my desk. How do I see myself sitting in the chair still peering at the bird while I'm up here? It feels infinitely good while being in the air. I would love to be able to fly as a bird being free and all of that. If I could fly, I wouldn't need a car or much money to go anywhere.

I feel it. A huge vacuum-like feeling starts pulling me towards the bird on my desk. The bird looks up at me as if knows something that I don't know. What's happening? Why am I'm being pulled towards this bird? I feel scared and excited all at the same time. I get the roller coaster stomach feeling as I'm pulled towards this bird.

We collide. It hurts. I take off like a helicopter; rocketing off my desk. Flying! Yes, flying! Am I a bird? Do I look like my normal self? Looking at where my arms and hands were, I see feather covered wings. I'm a bird. Why me? How me? I can still add, multiply and think like always, but I'm also enjoying free flight as a bird! Wow! But wait! I can't be a bird! This can't be real. What's going on? I can't be a bird. Imagine me, Donald Pecco, as a bird. What would Laura think? My family?

The headlines would read, "Man-bird found in Georgia". Please God, not a bird! It's so easy to fly. Flying around the city is so cool. Swirling masses of pink, plum-colored ashes float before my consciousness. There's nothing to life as a bird. No investments. No car or mortgage payments.

I land on the sidewalk in a park. The park is Central City Park in downtown. People seem to look at me in strange ways. I would think that as a bird, I would fit in with the other birds. Why am I being singled out? The park people are looking at me with such strange faces. Some are even laughing. Police come towards me with handcuffs. I see my reflection in the Georgia State government building's glass façade and see a horror worse than being a bird. I'm back to being a man, but I'm totally nude. How did I get in this situation?

How did I change from being a high and free flying bird to being a nude dude in the middle of a busy city park?

"No! Officers, I can explain! Please hear me out!" I run away from the encroaching police officers. I'm confused about why this is happening. I run up Peachtree Street. I run for what seems like hours and half days. The police officers are almost gaining on me. I'm tired and out of breath.

Oh no! I don't believe this! This is astronomical! But, how can it be?! I stop running. Peachtree stops at an immense hole. But not a hole, a crater. Crater. My mind searches for the word that means larger than crater. I see a miles deep depression. There's nothing on the other side of this massive hole. I would even surmise that this could be the end of (rinnnng!!) the earth.

Rinnnng!!!! Time to get up for work.

Sex Education: One day @ Pussy Tree

I spent my early years in Augusta, Georgia. An old city joining a section of Georgia and South Carolina together; a city blessed with a bunch of hospitals, the 'Big Golf Game,' and the Savannah River. In this big small city, my imagination was my only true friend. I remember the fun times going to my aunt's house during the summer. I was maybe seven or eight years old when I first noticed the tree.

Only my imagination could see what I saw on that tree. At that age, I could not have possibly seen a real one or even know what a real one looked like. Nevertheless, I saw it and I showed it to my younger sister and cousin. There it was shaped by nature and having almost perfect form. This tree growing beside my aunt's house right next to her crooked driveway had what looked like a big pussy on it.

I do not exactly remember when I became pussy conscious. But that tree sported a big pussy and the other thing about it, the pussy was closed as if suggesting that it was a virgin pussy. Of course, I am interjecting my present views about it looking like a closed virgin pussy. I did not know what a virgin was and surely would not have known if a virgin pussy looked any different from any other kind of pussy. Playing near the pussy tree brought snickers to my sister, cousin, and me. For a long time we knew this was our major secret.

The illusion of this secrecy was shattered on one hot, nasty summer day. One of my older cousins and my daddy's stepfather's son had a secret to share with me. I was thirteen years old, eighty percent nerd and twenty percent cool. Walking across the street, I wondered what these sneaky-eyed dudes had up their sleeves. My imagination kicked in with fast car speed. Maybe I am being initiated into a club. Naw, I thought, I'm just being led to the pussy tree.

The grins on their faces got bigger as we got closer to the tree. My uncle usually talked loud, so when he adopted a hush, 'I'm full of secrets talk' vibe, I knew that this was not an ordinary gathering. I felt that I was being initiated into a world from which

I would never escape. In his best impersonation of a sneaky character, he pointed to the pussy shape on the tree and asked me if I knew what it was.

My cousin, with an equally sneaky freaky look on his face, started snickering. My uncle was not too much older than I was, but because my family put a lot of respect and dignity into the word uncle and in the person, an uncle had almost as much respect as a father. In my young silly mind, my respect for my uncle was put in another category. Any mystery that he had as an uncle was destroyed, and at the same time, I felt a little fear. I started to feel that I was being initiated into the 'you're getting older' club. I had a bad taste in my mouth from my fears. I knew what I thought the shape on the tree looked like, but did I know what it was.

Was I being set up to be laughed at? Were my uncle and cousin just asking an obviously sexually inexperienced boy about an intimate female body part that they surely must've seen many times, to hear my response and fall out laughing?

Well, I summoned the courage to tell them that it was a pussy. I heard a slight giggle from the right. I then felt lightheaded and a little hungry. My uncle then asked me if I had ever screwed one. Now this question really took me by surprise. Screwed one? Do they realize that I am only thirteen? Thirteen year-olds do not screw pussies to my knowledge. We only liked to hump on girls' booties and if we got lucky, we could "get the front side".

I felt an overpowering urge to tell them that I had screwed a pussy before, feeling a little like an initiate of their club. I was in a nervous, silly teen mood. I allowed the word yes to slide out of my innocent mouth. My cousin jumped into overdrive with his questions about my pussy getting experience. Why would he ask that? I starting drawing on serious imagination, some of my lies came to me from the sneaky readings of my mother's sex education book.

After the first word or two out of my mouth, my uncle knew I was a virgin. So, we walked into my aunt's den and I, the student was given a whirlwind sex education. It was straightforward and strangely enough, it seems as if my mother, grandmother, and aunt knew about this whole scene unfolding. My mind started its thing of non-stop questions. Did my mom and the others ask my uncle and cousin to drag me to the pussy tree just to initiate this informal 'University of Sexual Education'? Of course, my young silly ass could not be without nervous embarrassed laughter with each description of the sexual events.

The turning point came when my uncle told me about condoms. He told me that I should put these on my dick to keep from making a baby. He told me about an internal stream that would shoot out of my dick when the sex is feeling the best. I knew about the mechanics of that from reading my mom's black sex book.

But I had never experienced the stream when humping on girls around that time. I knew that the humping felt good, but why didn't my stream shoot out? I started to feel that maybe the stream would only come out if I put my dick in a pussy. Somehow I was confused about the sex mechanics, not connecting what I had been doing in humping is essentially the same as screwing, except my dick would be in her instead of in my underwear or on her booty.

The lessons lasted for a while. My mother walked in with an "I know what you're talking about" look on her face. She looked at my uncle and cousin and verified my suspicions with the question of "are y'all teaching that boy about the birds and bees?" By now, I am through, my mother knows! This cannot be happening. My uncle answered. "He'll be cool."

It was almost two years before I actually got me some, and yes my inside stream flowed out and yes, I did have a condom on. Strangely, for the first few times that I screwed, those lessons in my thirteenth year would whisper in my ear when it was time to perform. I would then grin in the dark while mounted on top of some man's daughter.

Many years later, I visited pussy tree a few times with my first wife and then my second wife. I felt that the showing of this tree was like showing them a sacred object or something serious like that. Both times, they listened to my story, while being in awe about the way nature carved this pussy into the tree. Even though things did change, I'll never forget my nasty, sun summer day schooling that broke the secret of pussy tree, and what started me on the road to the serious study of how and at what cost I could get mo' pussy because I liked to feel the inside stream shooting out.

Troubled Innocence

"Maybe it will rain today," says Christine.

"Well, I don't know, the weatherman said that it was supposed to clear up later", replied her man.

"Christine, are you thinking about your man again? Christine?"

Christine can't keep her mind on her teacher's lessons or on anything for that matter. "Her man." Just think, that's what the other girls say about Kevin. That's Christine's man. I want everything to be just right when me and Kevin have our outing in the park Saturday.

Christine is a pretty teenager of forbidden energy. With thick naturally golden curls with a touch of purple as her grandfather say all the time. This time Christine looks as if she has butterflies in her stomach. Her best friend Sharonda tries to probe her.

Sharonda is a different sort of girl. She's in a different classification all together. She's sort of a momma type and best friend at the same time. Girls like Sharonda usually know something's not right with people and she wants to know what's up with Christina.

"Well Sharonda, promise me you won't tell anybody this."

"Tell anybody what?" Sharonda asked.

"Sharonda, I can't tell you, you won't promise."

"Okay Christy, I won't tell anybody."

"Sharonda, you must promise."

"Okay Christy, I promise not to tell anybody."

"Sharonda, I'm scared to death!"

"Scared of what?"

"I'm scared to go to the park with Kevin."

"Why are you scared to go to the park with your boyfriend of three months?"

"Sharonda, there's something I've never told you about me. Sharonda, I'm a... a virgin."

"You're a virgin?! What about all of these guys that you slept with in the past two years? You mean you were lying to me all of this time?"

"You see um, Sharonda why I was hesitant to telling you; I mean you're like a sister, a best friend all rolled up into one. I didn't want to hurt you. Please forgive me for lying."

"Okay Christy, now that you've spilled your guts on that subject, did you need any advice on your first time?" Sharonda tried her best to hide the big grin forming on her face. Christine noticed the grin and felt a little embarrassed, but managed to squeak out the words, "well sort of, but I'm afraid."

"Christy, how do you feel about Kevin?"

"I guess I really love him."

"Have you ever tried to have sex with any other guy before?"

"Yes about two years ago, his name is Bobby Peterson. He kinda hurt me all over. It was too big."

"Well Christy, some guys, especially younger guys don't have much experience or the patience to deal with a virgin. I had the luck of being with a guy in his 20's when I was broken in. I fell in love with him and never saw him after that night. I cried. Cried like a baby for several days."

'Sharonda, do you think Kevin is going to leave me after he gets what he wants?"

"Well, it's like this Christy; it depends on how Kevin feels about you. I mean, does he care about you or what?"

"Well, he says that he cares about me very much, but never said he loves me. He's never really pestered me for sex either."

"Does he know that you are a virgin?"

"Well, um...no. That's the other scary part. I don't want him to think that I'm not ready for him. I feel that I'm ready and want him to be inside of me very badly."

"Well, Christy, the only thing I can tell you is, just talk to him about you being a virgin and tell him that you're ready to be with him in that way. You should also stress to him that you've already tried, unsuccessfully, to have sex before. By stressing this to him, you immediately set a challenge for him to outdo the other guy by being gentler and successfully completing the break in." Sharonda almost burst out laughing after saying the words "break in".

"I'm still kinda scared, but I feel a lot better since earlier today. Thanks Sharonda, I love you!"

"I love you too Christy."

Park day. Not a holiday or even a birthday. It's my day. My day. It didn't rain like I hoped and Kevin said. The door bell chimes. It must be Kevin. Christine opens the door to find her man standing on the other side smiling.

"Oh Kevin I missed you so much."

Kevin. Medium brown complexion with a rebel guy haircut from the 1960's. Kevin is an intellectual human structure. A structure made out of a little bit of jealousy, love, and a lot of genius. Christine and Kevin are walking hand in hand or is it hand n hand.

Nearing a huge rose bush, Kevin plants a huge kiss on Christine's lips. Her lips are smallish, crescent moon thin and moist. His lips are thicker and not as moist. Whenever Christine is with her man, she feels faint, but not faint as in falling out faint, but faint as in the world fades into him. Everything slowly crystallizes into him. It's getting a little darker now. But I want to be in the dark says Christine to herself.

As Christine and Kevin walk more into the park, Christine scopes out every hiding place, every nook and cranny where the act can take place. They find a nice little cozy nook in a more secluded wooded area of the park. Now we can do it, Christine thinks.

Wait! What if Kevin doesn't want to do it? He may be a virgin. Kiss. I love the feel of a thick tongue slithering around the inside of my mouth. As he lay on top of me, I parted my legs to allow his hardening pack to press against my throbbing self.

Kevin's hands explore Christine's body with the skill of an archeologist. First layer of clothing off. Kevin can't help but to observe Christine's beautiful body. Nice thick thighs and wide hips. His hands slide under her round plump booty. As he squeezes her bubble booty, his erection increases to the point where Christine sees it through his underwear.

Christine starts to feel possessed when he caresses between her legs. She feels embarrassed because of the wet spot in her panties that's fed by her yearning body and mind. Christine tells him that she loves him so much and that she has never done it before, but wants to do it with him now.

"Please be gentle with me Kevin. Don't hurt me; it's happened before about two years ago."

Kevin promises that he won't hurt her and says that she'll come back to have sex with him. He slides off her panties and starts rubbing her down there softly. Softly. As he gently fingers her, she lets out a slight sigh and she lifts up a little only to relax. He licks a finger and put one inside her-gently. She gets wet and has a slight sweet odor.

Christine never imagined that this could feel this good and without pain.

"Kevin, put it in. I want it Kevin."

Kevin slid it in and started humping slowly while rolling his hips and thrusting. She couldn't believe it. She was actually having sex. Real sex. It feels good! Moments later, Kevin let out a low moan. His body got tense and then he went limp.

"Are you okay baby?" asked Christine.

"Yes. Yes. I came."

Kevin pulled out of Christine. Sticky stuff. Smells weird.

"It's me" says Kevin. "You don't have to worry about anything Christine, you won't get pregnant. We didn't do it long enough to worry about that."

Next Day

"Sharonda, I did it! I can't believe it! I did it last night in Hopkins Park."

"How was it girl?"

"It was nice. It was nothing like two years ago. He was very gentle with me. After he came in me..."

"Came in you?! Christy, you mean you let him come in you? Girl, do you realize you can get pregnant? Did he use a condom?"

"No, but he said that I wouldn't get pregnant because we didn't do it very long."

"You didn't do it very long?! Length of time has nothing to do with you being able to get pregnant. I've had a couple of friends that got pregnant after sex for mere seconds."

Five Weeks Later

"Sharonda, I didn't get my period yet."

"When does it usually come on?"

"It should have come last Monday."

"Oh shit Christy, we need to get you a pregnancy test."

"I can't be pregnant, not me; Christine Evans, a straight A student from the good side of the tracks. I can't stand Kevin! He did this to me. Knowing what he knew, I hate him."

It says here that if the paper turns blue, then I'm pregnant. Stay green. Stay white. Any color except blue. A thousand hours passed by-still no change. At the ten thousandth hour, the paper turned as blue as the sky. Please God don't let this happen to me. Christine started to cry on Sharonda's shoulder.

"I knew I shouldn't have done this. How could you let me do this Sharonda? It's all Kevin's fault."

"No Christy, don't blame Kevin, blame me. If I hadn't given you that half advice on sex, you would have been better prepared. I'm sorry Christine."

"Sharonda, what am I gonna do? I can't tell my parents about this."

"Well Christy, we don't have many options, actually we have only two."

"Two? What are they?"

"Either you tell your parents about this and they will help you prepare for the baby or..."

"Prepare for the baby?! Sharonda don't you realize that they'll prepare for my funeral. I can't tell them. What's the other choice?"

"Well Christy, the other choice is dangerous."

Dangerous. A word that was not associated with girl talk. Dangerous. A word that doesn't even feel good being in the same sentence as sex, pregnant and baby.

"Christy have you ever heard of abortions?"

"Abortion? Well, yes and no. I've heard of the word, but I don't know what it means."

"Christy, abortion is the ending of a fetus' life, which is the small form growing inside you. I remember reading about it in one of my history classes. Back in the 2020's, there was a major debate between people that opposed abortion, they called themselves "pro-lifers" and the people that believed that abortion should remain legal as it had been since the early 1970's."

"Sharonda, why the history lesson? Some of ..."

"Christy listen up. Abortion was ultimately made illegal, I think in 2022 after lengthy and costly court battles between the pro-lifers and the people who were for abortion. I think they called themselves "pro-choice". The pro-lifers won and now no one can get an abortion unless the woman's JobTrak will make it impossible to raise the baby to today's standards."

"So if it's not legal anymore, how can I get one done?"

"That's the part I was getting to. It can be done and of course it's illegal and dangerous as hell."

"I'm almost afraid to ask about the procedure and how it's done."

"Most people use clothes hangers."

"Clothes hangers?!"

"Yes, to pull it out of you."

"Oh that's gross. I'm scared Sharonda. Is it that dangerous Sharonda?"

"Yes, a lot of women have lost their lives doing the procedure."

A Week Later

"Sharonda, I can't tell my parents about my being pregnant. I have to get rid of it. But I'm scared."

"Christy, I know somebody that can help you. She's done this for at least five years."

"Has anybody ever...?"

"Christy, trust me, she's good."

"But wait Sharonda, you didn't let me finish."

"Christy, I said she's very good at what she does-please trust me, okay?"

"Sharonda, all I want to know if anybody's ever died during the procedure-her procedure?"

"Well Christy, it's like this..."

"No! Sharonda, I want to know; now-stop stalling me!"

"Okay, okay! Yes, two girls died out of maybe 250. I feel safe with that number enough to recommend my friend to you Christy."

"Do you think I should do it Sharonda?"

"Well, it's up to you Christy, but out of the people doing these operations; she's the best."

Another Week Later

"Hey Christy, meet me on Chester Boulevard around 4:30 tomorrow, Love Sharonda."

Chester Boulevard. Mom told me about that side of... The bell rang. Class is dismissed-Homework on American History, 1990's-2020's due tomorrow. As Christie boarded the #291 bus, she played scenes by her-bad scenes. Scenes only seen on the news or read about in the paper. Chester Boulevard. The street was wide with numerous potholes scattered about it. The people on the street seemed to be drug dealers. Newsflash: teenage girl dies of illegal abortion. No, No, please help me. Maybe I could talk to my parents about my pregnancy.

No, I must be crazy, especially how my mom reacted after I asked her a simple question about sex. She put me on punishment for a week. I must get on with this abortion so I can live peacefully after this. Live?! What if I don't live? What if my life is snuffed out by a hanger?

"Christy, I'm over here! Christy!"

Christine crossed the busy street to meet her friend. They walked down a side street filled with neat little houses. They arrived at Sharonda's friend's home.

"Are you sure you want to do this?" asked both females.

"Yes! Hurry, I want to get it over with."

Where am I? It feels strange, but good. So confused. Please God don't punish me for what I did. I don't want damnation. I don't want damnation. I like it here. I feel good here. Sharonda, can you see me? Can you hear me? I can see you. I'm sorry Sharonda I couldn't stay with you.

In today's top story: A teenage girl from Seaside Estates died this afternoon from complications from an illegal abortion performed on her. The perpetrator is still at large. Police thinks that this is the same person linked with the deaths of other abortion-girls in the past five years.

Fast Forward

There used to be simpler times. Times when dogs wouldn't back talk people and wives were considered super weak. But of course I'm stuck here, looking at this monstrous piece of machinery before me.

But, I dare not move, for if I should, I'd be pulverized to the smallest fraction of atom. Having the machine as the incarcerator instead of being in an old fashioned jail, is almost like being on "near death row", seems that the criminals and the accused had it better long ago. I hate this machine.

It wasn't always this way. At one time I enjoyed basic liberties that were enjoyed by the race in the other century. But they say they saw me in the girl's bedroom window raping her. This is something I wouldn't do as I had a girlfriend at the time. I wasn't sex starved. I don't believe in raping anyone to have sex.

Oh no, I twitched a little, will the Machine get me?

The last time I had non-Machine time, I didn't eat out of protest. I shouldn't even be here. I didn't do it! If the girl victim was of another design, I wouldn't be here. Yet I, the innocent, have to suffer because of the First Level Judging Panel's hatred of my kind. (Electronic voice speaks: Mr. Walker 6936, go to room B-10). Thank God it's time for non-Machine time.

I go into the room. It's filled with other first level judgments or people that were judged at the first level and who have to sit in front of the Machine until their judgment or what my great granddaddy would call their "court date". The environment and mood is one of loneliness and pathetic. I decide to eat something this time around, so I squeeze the round piece and wait on the internal juice to flow out. I then chunk it in my mouth. The taste of the round piece is a weird combination of dull and sweet.

One of the Society Intervention Officers (SIO) comes to me as I'm squeezing the last drop into my mouth.

"Mr. Walker, your judgment won't be coming up until six more months. Do you want the Fast Forward option or do you want to wait out the whole six months in front of the Machine?"

Keeping in mind that the Fast Forward option would cost me an additional 25,000,000 DOLs. But it would be worth every DOL.

"I want to do the Fast Forward option."

I reach over to the PrintScan to have the money deducted from my account, using my right thumb.

"Mr. Walker, follow me to the FF Room."

We walk into this room that's filled up with computers from floor to ceiling and it has a strong electrical smell; the kind that my great-grandfather told us about through the History Repeater, about his model train transportation sets when they would overheat.

I was strapped into this thickly padded chair and my face was covered with this warm gel-like substance. The SIO then placed these two small thin round metal objects above both of my eyes and slid a black cap-like cloth over the top of my head, just above my eyes. I felt a weird, tingling and "pushing" feeling when the cap touched the round metal objects. The SIO pressed a few buttons on the table in front of me and waved his hands across several computer screens. The chair began to rise slightly and vibrate slowly at first, then violently.

I remember one of my cousins telling me about the Fast Forward option. It's the alternative to having to sit in front of the machine for the duration of your incarceration and eventual judgment. Because I'm not officially judged, I don't think the Fast Forward option would be as scary as I'd heard my cousin say it was. I'm only doing it for six months. This is the lesser of two evils, I hope.

I must have been asleep for some hours now. What in the hell? Where am I? There was open space where the FF Room stood. There were no clouds, no buildings or trees. Where am I? What's going on? As I walked across the endless field, I noticed these strange looking plant-like things floating in the air. There were no birds or insects. Is this earth? I walked for eleven hours and the terrain did not change at all. There were no hills, valleys, rivers or people or other life forms (other than the floating plant creatures). I tried digging into the ground with my heel, only to find it virtually impossible. How can this be? What happened to the familiar earth creatures and terrain? I walked for a couple of hours and started getting tired.

My shoes seemed sluggish at my feet. I kept going for another 30 minutes. I found a spot that was not unlike the whole of where I've experienced in my more than half day walk. I will lie down and get some rest here. My pants felt that they were much larger than they were yesterday. My shoes were larger too. I'm so confused by this. Why are my clothes so much larger today?

It didn't matter...yawn.

When I awoke a few hours later, I was lying next to a huge object. It wasn't a boulder or a landform as it felt like leather. It didn't have the familiar irregular natural forms of earth. It seemed to be made by man. I walked around this huge "leather boulder". This is...my...shoe?! But how can it be? The growing shoes and clothes were actually me shrinking. It seems that I've become much smaller, perhaps 30 or 40 times smaller. Why did this happen?

Suddenly a huge shadow was cast over me. The floating plants! The plants were huge and more menacing. Why are they slowing down near me? They are turning around towards me. They're coming at me! I try to run, but I must get from under what were my clothes and are now like a house sized fabric.

I run as fast as I could into the horizon-less void. They're gaining on me. The beige one has a huge scoop at the end of its tentacle and this tentacle is on the ground, coming after me, gaining ground.

I'm sucked into this thing! There's a lot of hair everywhere. I start to fall. Now I fall long and fast. Falling and more falling. I fall for what seems like two hours. Now it feels as if my fall has slowed down, even stopped. This is so confusing. I find myself in this huge room with a few people.

"Mr. Walker, your judgment has been moved up and is ready one day after you went into FF. Come forth. After hours of Second Level Judging; you are found guilty of rape. Mr. Walker, you're sentenced to two years under the Machine or you can choose the Fast Forward Option...for two years."

Animal

The bacteria, viruses and parasites (the Microscopics) have been in existence for a few billion years. Over time, they coexisted with the new earth creatures in a sort of passive aggressive pushing and pulling for survival which has worked over several millennia.

Man later came on the scene, and over a period of hundreds of thousands of years has managed to disrupt earth's living systems, eventually disregarding the delicate life design as well as humanity's innate actions that would help insure their survival. Now humans have to create committees and non-profits to consciously think about their survival.

The Microscopics all evolved to some level of advanced neural development, or a rudimentary brain. While this allowed for communication between the Microscopics, this sub group wouldn't be able to communicate with another Animal subgroup until starting about 100 years ago.

With eventually knowing of humanity's propensity for slow destruction of their once perfect environment, the Microscopics formed the goal of stopping the human sub group from increasing their numbers, also known as the Human Threat or Threat. Because of this new found urgency, the Microscopics had to initiate communication with the next life form up from them: the Multicellulars. After a short period of much chaos within both subgroups, peace finally was achieved between the groups in AD 1952.

The two groups, now a unified front, attempted communications with the Crawlers. The initial attempts were met with mass feedings on the Microscopics and Multicellulars until the higher evolved Crawlers allowed communication between the groups. This happened in AD 1958.

The Threat has intensified over the past couple of decades with the atmosphere losing some of the good gases and gaining too much of the bad gases. It was more important than ever for the three animal groups, who are now calling themselves the Lower Forms; to discuss bringing in other entities. At this point, they communicated about the need to get the Watery and Earthy groups on board.

The initial communication attempt was met with much feeding on the Lower Forms and chaos for about three years. Eventually, peace ensued and the Watery and Earthy groups along with the Microscopic, Multicellulars and Crawlers formed a pact in AD 1962.

Although the Microscopics have created several Events over millions of years, some of their most artistically creative Events have been the Black Death, Bubonic Plague, the 1918 Flu and into more recent Events such as AIDS. These Microscopic Events caused major depletions of Human stock, this exemplified how well the Microscopics communicated to start the Campaign against the Threat.

Since 2024, humanity has been in steady decline because of what many of the uninitiated among the humans are calling the Apocalypse, but the more enlightened underground communities are calling this an attack from earth itself. Every day, there are stories about house pets killing their owners, more wild animal attacks and killings and there's a new disease that's transmitted by snow and ice storms. This disease for some strange reason will only kill unborn humans.

This is the year 2060, all Creatures born since 2016 have been born with one thing, awareness and that is to destroy the Threat. The Threat was identified long ago and the Creatures' response to this Threat has been a meticulous Campaign which ensured their success by being as far in the background as to not arouse any suspicion from Humanity. Their campaign which was launched less than 200 years ago, has managed to deplete human stock to where their population is now only 3 billion, down from a high of 10 billion in the 2040's.

With fewer Humans on the earth, there's been a seven fold increase of the Creatures' populations and with this increase; Humanity will eventually be eliminated in a few decades.

The Office Building

Today was a different day at the office. My boss and I didn't engage metaphysically, in sex. I've given my life to the company, well at least 78% ownership of it.

The building, there's something about the building. On floor 17, this man leases his wife out to the company for 7800 credits a month. They make good credits, but it's something about this building that puts that thing in my head and in the other's heads.

One Globe Federation-Atlantanooga, caught these old fashioned freaks, freaking on the lobby garden roof, don't they know that they just can't do that anymore?

It was banned along with cigarettes and meat several years ago.

This building is kinda freaky, I mean, look at the way it looks similar to open female legs, for the male member to penetrate, and it does.

There's this subconscious thing making me want to freak her, but in the old way. It's the building, so vertical and freaky. It virtually tells me to freak against the law.

The next day, infinitely different, I freaked. My boss, she was freedom on the 29th floor. We freaked and licked and I shot her insides out.

With the freak smell alert system, they got us. Our pictures were splattered on the ComNet.

I know it's the building. It's a freaky building.

Technology

"But momma, I wanna watch Scooby Doo!!"

"Listen, if you don't get outta making all that noise, I'm gonna get you!"

Television. America's most addicted drug. Without it, the mother would surely die. Staples, the Scooby Doo addicted son went into his tiny bedroom and turned on his stereo. This almost MENSA genius boy was a fan of the 60's rock group, The Jefferson Airplane.

His room is a statement in itself; with pictures of his favorite girls on one wall, while another wall hosts his bizarre drawings of three headed children. Something about pyramids has fascinated this small kid for much of his life. Pyramids.

Sometimes this Staples kid would spend hours reading about the ancient Egyptian Mysteries system, learning about...what?

Even my friends started noticing it the other day. It started with a low hum. After a few days, this hum grew louder and more pronounced.

"Staples, leave the channel alone, I'm watching my show!"

Nine days later, all of our plants had died. Pure dead.

Staples' mom sat there focusing on the moving images on the screen while the hum grew louder; but she never noticed. Hummmmm.

"Staples, where are you? Staples come here."

She thought that she remembered this commercial, but it didn't seem the same. Something was added, or missing. Hummmm. She sat, waiting on her show. Hummmm.

Slowly, a geometric pattern emerged in the bottom left corner of the screen. The T.V. went silent. Momma, tried turning the

T.V. on, but nothing happened. She knew someone that could come over tomorrow and fix it, but she would miss her show tonight.

The next day the T.V. repairman showed up. "How strange, this T.V. is practically brand new. Cal, what would cause this to happen?"

Cal replied in a tone of confusion, "I've never worked on a T.V. with this type of problem before, but I know someone that could fix it. If he can't, no one can. The only thing is I won't be able to reach him until next week."

Staples had been bringing some of the strangest friends to the house over the past few days and he seemed pretty laid back about the whole T.V. affair. Maybe he's happy that his mom hasn't controlled the set in the past week.

I was sitting there when it happened! Honest! We sat in the living room while the stereo was playing. Of course the T.V. is still not working; and then it happened. Suddenly out of nowhere, the music coming out of the stereo starting playing very fast; as if it was playing at 10 times the normal playing speed.

The same geometric pattern reappeared in the same place on the dead T.V. screen. The humming of last week came back, but the sound was like that of an electronic coding or some weird Morse code-ish sound.

Mom got caught! The T.V. pulled her into itself!

"Mom! Mom! Where are you?!!"

I couldn't see her, but I heard more of that weird electronic coding sound mixed with a high pitch electro screaming sound. After a couple of minutes, it grew quiet. Terror. I was terrified so much that my eyes were transfixed on the screen and I couldn't move.

Suddenly, the same geometric pattern appeared on the screen. I mustered enough energy to pull away from the menacing scene and run into the kitchen. I noticed a hum nearby. Looking over my shoulder, I noticed that the microwave had the same geometric pattern displayed on its face. What's going on? It doesn't *feel* right here. I run into the bathroom, shutting and locking the door.

I started rationalizing about the increasingly eerie situation and laughed aloud, "What am I locked in here for? What could a T.V. and microwave do to me?" I felt foolish for seemingly overreacting to what may be an electrical problem in the house.

The lights went dim, then back to normal brightness, then dim again and back to normal. At this point, I knew this had to be an electrical problem, but what happened to my mom? I saw... The hum is back and seems to be coming from the bathroom.

The tub was clear. The sink was empty. I slowly opened the door.

A most terrible sight greeted me when I opened the door. This was terror to the nth degree. The T.V., microwave, stereo and two lamps were just outside the bathroom door. A split second, no a split millisecond, I slammed the bathroom door shut, locking it. Something was weird or felt weird. It felt like a combination of static and pressure.

How did the devices get there? What's going on? My mind was racing in circles. An hour went by. The silence was killing me. Mind racing. What did these devices want? They're outside this door as if they're coming for me.

Pop! The loud popping sound took me by surprise and fueled my increasing and already out of control fears about the assemblage outside the door. What in the world was that sound?

I hear a shuffling, moving sound near the bottom of the door. What the...? Three cords are sliding under the door, coming into the bathroom.

I stepped back, not knowing if the cords will grab my feet or send some electrical energy under the door. I couldn't take any chances. I then noticed it. It was even more horrible than the other stuff combined! This is not real, I must be dreaming. No, I must be in a nightmare. Growing out of my left hand was an electronic resistor.

Funny Train

One cold brisk day (many stories start this way), on this particular morning, I was to meet my friend at the train station. Without seeing my coworker, friend or whatever; I got back on the train.

On the train, there are many people, different colors and shapes, all looking at some fixed personal point in space. The train began to slow, go slower until it stopped between stations. Yes, the void, no man's land, secret passageway.

In that moment, the announcer announces "next station Midtown station." A few chuckles, cackles and guffaws stung the nonchalant air with the feel of a circus.

Making Them Money

My job is a scene. The people can be nice or mean depending upon the position of the week. My presence there can be both a disturbing one as well as an entertaining one. Most of the employees/workers are top level thinkers with the same goals of becoming successful/ rich.

Complaints here and there sprinkle the damp undertones of working for the scene makers.

Marriage

What are deep thoughts? Comparing and illustrating for a common thought. Marriage is a union with paper and family. In many cases that union ends with dirty paper.

Triangle

A triangle is really a parallelogram where one side is missing-- possibly stolen.